Fire Bright

AMY LAURENS

OTHER WORKS

Find other works by the author at www.amylaurens.com

Fire Bright

INKLET #61

AMY LAURENS

Inkprint PRESS

www.inkprintpress.com

Print ISBN: 978-1-922434-61-6
eBook ISBN: 9798201187972

www.inkprintpress.com

National Library of Australia Cataloguing-in-Publication Data
Laurens, Amy 1985 –
Fire Bright
68 p.
ISBN: 978-1-922434-61-6
Inkprint Press, Canberra, Australia
1. Young Adult Fiction—Fantasy—Dark Fantasy 2. Young Adult Fiction—Fantasy—Romance 3. Young Adult Fiction—Short Stories, Collections & Anthologies

First Print Edition: July 2021
Cover photo © Enrique Meseguer via Deposit Photos
Cover design © Inkprint Press
Interior art © Amy Laurens

FIRE BRIGHT

THE FOURTH TIME SHE WOKE IN THE night, hot, wet, and buzzing slightly all over from the lingering effects of the dream, Adela was forced to admit that she had a problem.

It was wartime. People were dying. She and Bug and Leroy were on a mission to save the world—literally, if somewhat melodramatically at times —and yet all she could think about in her spare time, all she dreamt about while sleeping, was Jiri.

That was first of all a bad thing because Jiri was a jerk and she hated him and she resented him taking up her mental real estate like this.

But also it was also a bad thing because—and this was the unfortunate bit—of what Jiri was *doing* in her dreams.

There was a reason she'd woken up hot and bothered, and it wasn't because the dream had been *bad*.

Which was, of course, the worst part: dream Jiri was a superlative lover—not that, at seventeen, she'd had any real-life experience to compare him to—and that just added to her resentment.

And made the problem all the harder to ignore, because she hadn't *had* any real-world experience in that department, so what the *hell* was her brain thinking here? Where was it coming *up* with this stuff?

Which made the problem even *worse*, because—and this was the bit she wanted to admit to least—what if her brain *wasn't* just making this stuff up?

Jiri had freed her from his uncle's house a month ago. Had defected from the enemy to, presumably, Adela's own side. Had risked his life to get her out... But only after the Anamata had told him to.

Anamata, the famous, horrendously expensive potion that, when you drank it, gave you mild premonitions and the unerring ability to act in the way that best furthered your goals for the next six to twelve months, sometimes a little longer.

Anamata, which, it was rumoured, if you drank it in the right time, in the right place, with the right person, would show you your future together, whatever that might be.

Jiri had just *happened* to have some lying around, because of course you did when your family had gotten that filthy rich off the back of racism and inbreeding and old, old money, and he'd brought it into the filthy, squalid bedroom where his uncle had been keeping Adela prisoner, and Jiri had offered her a drink of the potion.

At five hundred thou a pop, and with the potential to save your life if 'survival' happened to be on your twelve-month to-do list, Adela had hardly been in a position to say no.

Especially when he'd told her that he was considering breaking her out, if the Anamata confirmed that was what he was supposed to do.

Bastard. Never mind just letting her go because it was the *right* thing to do.

Only—of course—there was no way to tell how much of what he'd said was the truth, because all sorcerers lied, and all sorcerers could tell when someone was lying.

All sorcerers, that was, except Adela.

On her camp mat in the dark in the four-person tent, sandwiched between Bug on her right and Leroy on her left because the middle was the warmest spot and who was she to argue with chivalry, Adela drew in a deep, shaky breath.

The air smelled warm and close, the boys' sweaty clothes from the day musting up the air—and Adela was going to have to get up and get changed, because the stupid dreams had left her damp.

So she peeled herself the rest of the way out of her bag and tiptoed to the door of the tent, goosebumps rising on her bare legs (she still couldn't deal with the idea of wearing pants to bed; leggings, maybe, if it was cold enough for frost, but otherwise, ew, no thanks, no way, she'd rather throw on an extra blanket than have her legs suffocated like that). Adela unzipped the door one slow inch at a time, heart pounding. *Don't wake up, don't wake up.* But she opened a gap large enough to slip through and stepped out into the fresh night air, stretching her arms up and arching her spine as she breathed more easily.

Ironically, out here she had less to worry about in terms of privacy; the closest person right now other than the boys in the tent was over fifty kilometres away. Still, though it was plenty warm enough to avoid a frost, the air nipped at her skin, making the goosebumps more pronounced. She skipped across the grass quickly to the supply tent next door so she could rummage for some clothes.

The clearing in the woods was really quite bright for the middle of the night; Adela glanced upward, a little surprised to see a full moon cresting over the treetops.

Was it really time for the full moon again?

Hurriedly, though, she glanced away, because the moonlight sifting down through the patchy clouds was blue and clear, almost like the glow of Anamata.

One day, she told herself with a clenched jaw as she slipped inside the supply tent, she was going to go more than a minute without thinking of the Anamata—or of Jiri.

"Screw Jiri," she muttered as she stood in the centre of the blue-and-silver walled tent, the light from the moon making it glow.

The supply tent was a little larger than the sleeping tent, probably built for six people, and the roof was high enough that Adela, at a touch over five foot, didn't have to stoop at all in the middle. Consequently—and because of the distinct lack of sweaty bodies, Adela excepting—the air in here was quite pleasant, smelling faintly of the leftover sausages they'd cooked over a fire for dinner. Which was probably not a good thing, because if Adela with her craptastic sense of smell could smell it, then any passing wild-life definitely could, and the last thing they needed was another wildlife raid. They'd lost a week's worth of food to one early on, and since then had been extra cautious.

Clothes. Clothes first, then she'd pull the sausages out and rewrap them, adding another couple of layers of plastic wrap to dull the scent.

Adela knelt at her duffle bag against one of the side walls and rummaged around for clean underwear—and, impulsively, a full set of clothes.

Of course, she considered as she stripped off, flashing back to something similar occurring in the dream, there was a third, worse option.

If it wasn't her subconscious (Because how the hell would it know what to do? She'd never even *seen* a naked male until the war had started and she'd ended up stuck out here in the middle of nowhere with two teenage boys who'd given up on notions of privacy when it became apparent that privacy involved a degree of effort nobody had after spending a full day running for your life)…

And if it wasn't the Anamata (because what on *earth* did having intensely *bothersome* dreams about Jiri have to do with 'furthering her goals' for the next year?)…

That meant it had to be Jiri himself, projecting into her dreams somehow, or implanting them, or something.

If that was the case, she was *actually* going to kill him, because the dreams —had she mentioned?—were hyper realistic, and she'd kind of always loosely harboured this crazy, outrageous idea that maybe she'd lose her virginity to someone of her choosing, and, you know, *in real life*.

Of course, *technically* she was probably still a virgin. (She pulled on a pair of jeans and a thin navy sweater and her tan walking shoes, because there was no way she was going back to sleep right now, ha ha, very funny, thanks for trying, come again later.)

But her body—or was it her brain? —certainly thought otherwise.

Adele ground her teeth. Her hands fisted at her sides and she marched out of the tent, barely pausing to zip it behind her before marching right out of the clearing where they were camped, and into the night-dark forest.

Around her, the trees—mostly oaks, with a smattering of ash—rustled and whispered. They seemed so much more alive at night, though whether that was just because there was less human noise competing with them or what, Adela couldn't say.

They definitely felt louder, though, more alive, like a slow-moving, slow-living alien species, intelligent, foreign, inhabiting the Earth but on a different time scale.

The rustling intensified, and Adela shrugged her shoulders against the discomfort creeping down her spine.

Something felt wrong.

A step before the magical protective barriers that she'd erected around their campsite, Adela paused.

Wait, the shushing leaves seemed to say. *Wait. Hold your breath.*

Okay, maybe she was finally starting to lose it under the strain of living in a battle zone, because that was a stupid thing to imagine trees saying. Hold your breath? What the—

Out there, in the darkness, something clicked.

Adela froze, rigid—and on the gentle night breeze, the smell of sulphur, like overly rotten eggs, drifted toward her.

Immediately, she drew in a quick breath and held it, sealing the back of her throat with the back of her tongue.

Scratch poison.

The trees had been right.

The skin behind her right ear itched, the soft part right behind her jaw bone, as a faint trail of gold and silver sparks whirled around her—just like brighter sparks had done when she'd drunk the Anamata with Jiri.

So. Not the trees. The potion, protecting her.

Slowly, slowly, breath still held and senses straining for the source of the poison, she sank to the ground, obeying the instincts of the premonitionary potion.

The pressure in her sinuses and throat built as her body fought to make her take a breath. Her chest began to tighten.

Hold! she told her body. *Hold it, or you'll die anyway!*

Tighter, tighter, until she began to ache… And before she could stop herself, her tongue moved, her throat unsealed, air rushed out of her and her body sucked a fresh breath in, fast and deep.

For a moment she cringed, waiting for the searing sensation of the scratch in her nostrils… But it didn't come.

It must have been nothing more than a stray gust on the wind, capable of stripping the lining from her airways, but transient, momentary, gone on the breeze as light as a moonbeam.

The Anamata had saved her.

On the ground, knees pressing into the leaf litter, damp seeping into her jeans, Adela buried her face in her hands.

The potion had saved her, and the potion was sending her dreams of Jiri.

"No," she muttered into the palms of her hands, lips brushing against her skin, palms cool in the night air. "I don't *want* that future."

Out in the woods, beyond the borders of her protective spells, a twig snapped.

Adela froze. It could have just been a normal nighttime noise, a spontaneous loss of a branch, the proverbial tree falling in the forest... Or it could have been a footstep.

Peering through her fingers, Adela stared through the trunks of the oaks —but the moonlight filtering through the clouds made shapes harder to see, edges blurring and shifting, her brain compulsively finding patterns that weren't there.

Another crack, followed by a rustle as something decent-sized brushed past a low-hanging branch.

There, ahead and to the right, something shifted in the dark.

Adela tensed, senses straining.

Slowly, the figure resolved: a person, taller than she was but thin, lanky, though with enough breadth in the shoulders to suggest a male she realised as they got closer.

And then he crossed a clear patch of moonlight, and Adela jerked back as though the boy had reached out across the intervening space and stung her, because she recognised that shock of blond hair gleaming in the night.

Eyes wide, Adela watched as Jiri drew closer, his own gaze sweeping back and forth through the trees intently as though searching for something.

A foot from the protective bubble around their campsite, Jiri stopped, staring at a place about half a foot to Adela's left.

She drew her knees up to her chest and watched him. The bubble would hold, she knew that from previous experience—it was pro-level spell-work, some of her best, designed to let air flow through naturally, but formed in such a way that it would capture sound waves as they travelled outward and balance out the movement, effectively acting as a one-way soundproof barrier.

So: she was safe to sit here and watch him. As long as she didn't stick an arm out through the barrier, he'd move on eventually, none the wiser as to what had made him suddenly stop and change direction.

It was hard to read the subtleties of his expressions in the simplifying moonlight, but she could certainly see the intensity of his gaze well enough—and she knew that his eyes, though generically dark right now, would have the look of a stormy ocean about them, deep, dark blue and laser focused.

She'd seen that look often enough at school, usually focused on some younger student who'd stumbled into his way.

A shiver shuddered through her; she was grateful that gaze wasn't focused on her.

"I know you're there," Jiri murmured suddenly, reaching out a hand toward her, if she'd been standing a foot to her left.

Adela glanced up to make sure there *wasn't* anyone there, then looked back at Jiri. What in the world?

"I can see the sparks," he said. "Gold and silver. Just like..." Slowly, he sank to the ground and crossed his long legs, his jeans scuffing and his rain-proof coat shushing.

His left knee was just about aligned with her own, three-ish feet in front of her. Adela hugged her legs tighter and rested her chin on her knees. What was he doing here? The Anamata had suggested that once they'd gone their separate ways in the woods last week, they wouldn't meet each other again until—

For a long time. So why was he here, now?

Her heart thudded. *Scratch poison.* Jiri's uncle was rumoured to have invented it—along with a whole bunch of other nasty weapons deployed in this vicious war. What if… What if that hadn't just been a stray gust of wind from some nearby guerrilla battlefront? He knew she was here, or guessed that someone was, at any rate.

What if he'd…

She swallowed. What exactly *were* his goals for the next twelve months, anyway?

Jiri exhaled heavily. "Okay, I get that you probably don't want to talk to me. That's fine. I'm just…" He glanced around and shifted awkwardly. "This is stupid," he muttered. "How do I know she's even there?"

He exhaled again and shook his head. "Look, Adela."

Adrenalin reared its head and looked around in her stomach; she didn't remember him ever using her first name before.

Had he called her Adela when he'd rescued her? She couldn't remember, but either way, it had been five and a half years of Gibson-this and Gibson-that. To hear him call her 'Adela' now was like a punch to the gut.

Adela pressed her face into her knees. Her jeans smelled like laundry powder. She inhaled deeply, and when Jiri stayed silent for a moment longer, looked back at him.

He was rubbing the back of his head, mussing up his hair—it was thick hair, left longer on top and shorter at the back and sides, and it tended to hold whatever position he'd last swept it into, and right now he was doing a great impression of a horned owl.

Adela had a brief flash back to one of the dreams, and sniggered at *horned*.

But Jiri, still oblivious to her presence—or, well, unable to see or hear her, at least—dropped his hands back into his lap, and glanced up at the place where, presumably, he could see the gold-and-silver sparks.

"I'm sorry, okay," he said, tone slightly aggressive, defensive, but carrying the unmistakeable hint of regret. "You don't know what it's like, to grow up with parents whose every move is calculated to indoctrinate a certain philosophy into you, who teach you that you're better than half the people on the planet, that things like respect and dignity are... are weakness."

He rubbed at his head again, and Adela felt herself coming a little undone. She wasn't *stupid*; she knew exactly what he meant, and how hard it must have been for him to start questioning the paradigm he'd been raised in.

But that didn't absolve him of being an asshole.

Jiri sighed heavily. "I was wrong. And I knew that in, like, fourth year, but that just made it worse, so I tried even harder to…" He stopped, took a breath, kept going cautiously like he was feeling out the words. "To win my parents' approval. Because I think by the end of fourth year, they were starting to suspect that I might cave on them. So fifth year was the worst, because I was trying to prove to them—to me—that they were right, and…" He shrugged awkwardly, then rubbed at his biceps. "I don't know how we're going to be together," he said. "How you could ever…"

One hand went to the back of his neck and he leaned his head against his raised arm, closing his eyes and sighing. "I don't know how to do this,

Adela," he said softly. "I know you hate me. You should. But…"

His gaze flicked back up, and this time, accidentally, because he'd shifted a little or because the sparks had or something, his gaze lit directly on Adela's face, and she gasped just a little.

"Anamata is never wrong, Adela. I didn't know it would show us what it did, and I'm sorry, and if there was any way I could change it, I would, because you deserve better than…" He made a flippant up-and-down gesture at himself with both hands, his eyebrows raised, then fell silent, forehead resting against three fingers.

Adela's heart was pounding, and her fingers hurt from digging into her jeans. It sounded plausible, it all did, but… Sorcerers *never* told the truth. Which sounded like a simple truism, but it was more than that: in a world where literally everyone could tell when you lied and when you spoke the truth, culture had decided that—humans being humans—it would be easier to pretend that this power didn't exist.

No sorcerer could switch their power off, but it had become a cultural agreement as ironclad as a prohibition on casual murder: everybody lied. All the time. About everything.

If you never told the truth, your lie-seeking senses would be constantly running low-grade interference, like white noise, and it would be the next best thing to not having the power at all.

Sorcerer children were trained in the fine art of letting people know what they wanted without ever telling the outright truth from the day they learned to talk.

And Jiri had come from a long, long line of exceptionally talented sorcerers—and liars.

Anamata might not lie—but then again, it was only ever sorcerers that had indicated that it didn't, so who knew what it did really?

He was here, after all; he knew basically where she was. Dreamcasting was complicated, high-level spellwork, but he'd been involved in some awful things last year, which he'd alluded to just now, and he was probably capable of it.

She hadn't thought to make the bubble dream-proof. So it was plausible that he was casting them, that he'd been the one with the scratch poison just now, that—

A horribly familiar sound whirred through the trees, angry and something like a far-distant chainsaw.

Instinctively, Adela threw herself to the ground—right as Jiri did, right as the red-glowing, magic-loaded bullet whirred through the place where Jiri's heart had been a fraction of an instant before, piercing him instead through the shoulder and exploding into fragments of light, each one burning at thousands of degrees and hovering, suspended, in the air, an angry sphere of torment around the place where the bullet had landed.

Jiri screamed.

Another bullet whirred toward him, this one from a different trajectory.

Adrenalin lit Adela's veins.

The bubble would stop them, she'd designed it specifically with things like this in mind, she was fine, she was safe…

And Jiri was screaming in agony in front of her as the second bullet missed him by a hair—probably fired before he threw himself down, which probably saved his life.

Bloody Anamata.

Adela scrambled forward, the musty, wet smell of leaf litter thick in her face, the whirring of more magic bullets loud enough in the night that they might as well have been fighter jets—just as angry, and at this exact moment, just as dangerous.

Adela reached the bubble, its elastic resistance like forcing her hand under a particularly heavy mattress.

One hand.

Her head.

Her other arm.

A bullet landed on the bubble right next to her and exploded. Pain lanced her ear.

Adela hissed. She lunged forward, grabbing Jiri around the chest, awkwardly hooking her arms under his.

Another bullet exploded in the leaf litter beside them, its periphery just setting fire to her knee.

More whirring.

A trail of firelight through the night.

Adela shrieked and ducked, burying her face in Jiri's side.

Jiri still hadn't stopped screaming.

Surely the boys would have heard something by now, Bug at least, and he'd wake Leroy, and they'd be on their way.

She just had to get Jiri back into the bubble.

Adela heaved, but it was like hauling on a tree trunk. She needed her feet under her. Urgh.

Quickly, she set Jiri back down. She stood, planting her feet and shaking out both hands in front of her. Major protective spells usually took her some time and preparation, but they'd been dodging around the edges of this war for five months now as they tried to piece together the information needed to find, identify and disable the other side's major weapon: a quick-and-dirty shield had been high on the list of priorities to learn.

Adela threw her head back, shaking her dark brown hair back from her face.

Red-gold bullets were whirring at her from at least three different directions, maybe more.

The bubble had her back.

Moonlight bathed her from above. The leaf litter grounded her below.

Adela drew on the power of the living organisms in the dirt below her feet, and let it pulse through her toward the moonlight. The two organic powers, light and life, met, and Adela snapped the resulting tangle of power out in front of her, a half-sphere shield that smelled like dirt after rain and glowed like the light of the moon.

Bullets peppered it, exploding into small, fire-bright stars.

But the shield held.

Left hand extended to maintain the flow of power, Adela stooped awkwardly and got her other arm under and around Jiri's shoulders where he lay on the ground.

No good. She couldn't move him like that, he was heavier than her and a dead weight.

"Jiri," she said, gaze flickering between his pale face and the streams of bullets now focusing to a point on her shield as the three shooters worked together to try to break through. "Jiri!"

He opened his eyes, found hers. He stopped screaming, breaths coming in ragged, heaving gasps.

"You have to help me," she said desperately. "Push with your legs. I have to get you back through the shield."

His face was tight, screwed up against the pain, tears flooding down his face, but he nodded, one brief jerk, and got his knees up.

"On three," Adela said. "One... Two... Three!" She pulled, wincing at his weight, at the fire beginning in her raised hand as the fireworks of the bullets began to break through.

Jiri pushed against the dirt, sliding along on his back toward the bubble—and screaming, clutching at his injured shoulder.

"I'm sorry," Adela panted. "I'm sorry. One more. Just one more."

Her heart thudded in her chest like it was going to break her ribs. Her stomach knotted.

A bullet broke through the shield, exploding as it did, sending sparks of fire into the tips of her left three fingers.

She shouted.

Jiri convulsed against her arm.

"Okay," she breathed, panting, hurting.

Another bullet broke through the shield and detonated, thankfully missing her.

The shooters were getting closer.

"Okay, okay." She shifted her grip on Jiri, her back aching from the awkward way she was crouched with one arm under him, her other arm up and holding the shield. Sweat covered her face, her lips salty with the taste of it, and the air smelled like burning matches.

"One."

Jiri tensed, panting too.

"Two."

Adela tensed, gripping his shirt in her fingers.

"Three."

He pushed, screaming.

She tugged, shouting as a third bullet came through and caught her hand in raging fire.

But then there was the feeling of sinking elasticity, the cool wash of the bubble checking her identity—and the bubble closed around them.

Bullets exploded against it, now-harmless fireworks in the night.

Jiri was curled around his injured shoulder, sobbing.

Adela cradled her left hand to her chest, squeezing it, knotting and un-knotting her fist as though it might ease the burning.

It wasn't the first time she'd been hit in this war, and it didn't hurt any less—but she'd learned—she'd *had* to learn—not to let the pain turn into panic.

She sucked air in through her teeth and forced it out through pursed lips.

Still hurt like a bitch, though.

Behind them, footsteps came, running through the leaves.

"Adela?"

She sank to the ground, the shakes of shock beginning. "Here," she called to Bug, and watched him adjust his course slightly as he heard her, saw the magic bullets screaming and whirring at the wall of the bubble.

"Security breach," Adela said as Bug raced to her. "This one's been hit," she added, jerking her head at Jiri.

Bug started, eyes growing wide, so much so that she could see it in the dim light. "Jiri."

"Yeah."

If there had been no love lost between Adela and Jiri during school, there had been more than hatred spilled between him and Bug.

"He's on our side, Bug," Adela said from the ground as she flexed and unflexed her hand.

Leroy crouched beside her. "Are you hurt?"

Adela held out her hand to him, and he folded it inside his. She shook her head. "Leave it. We need to break camp first before they find a way to break the bubble."

"What about him?" Bug said, still standing, staring at Jiri writhing on the ground as though he was some kind of poisonous worm.

Adela snorted, still panting, still gasping a little as Leroy wrapped one arm around her shoulders. "If I can wait, he can wait."

Bug nodded. "We'll pack the tents. We'll leave from here." He glanced up at the bubble, where bright fireworks were still cascading over it, red and gold like hungry tongues of flame, licking, searching, hunting. "We'll hurry, but we've got time before they break through."

Adela nodded. Swallowed. Gasped again. "Yeah," she said.

Leroy squeezed her gently.

"Go," she said. "Pack. We'll be fine here till you're ready."

Leroy nodded, stood, and he and Bug headed back to the tents at a run.

By her feet, Jiri curled up into a ball, shaking and trembling, but at least no longer shouting.

Adela doubted he'd ever felt anything like the fire that must be sparking through his shoulder right now, the points of light making a softball-sized sphere that was mostly embedded in his flesh.

He was doing alright.

Adela surveyed the bubble wall—but Bug was right. It was holding fast, as it was designed to. Bug and Leroy would have the tents packed and shrunk down in a matter of minutes. They be back, they'd all link up and vanish, and the bubble would deflate slowly over the next hour.

By the time whoever was out there got in, there'd be nothing left to say that anyone had ever been here.

Adela flopped backward, the cool of the leaf litter cradling her as she lay on the ground, the smell of dirt and clean decomposition enveloping her.

Above her, tiny gold and silver sparks floated back.

Adela scowled. "No," she told them. "I did what any decent person would do. That doesn't mean that he's my future."

Above her, the lights winked, and faded into the night.

THE MAKING OF
FIRE BRIGHT

In November of 2018, Liana Brooks wrote a cute, hot little enemies-to-lovers thing that will probably never see the light of day, unless I somehow end up rich enough to bribe her to finish it. It was, however, glorious, with very distinct Dramione* vibes, and the party scene for whatever reason was very lush in my mind.

So lush, in fact, that it called into being an alternate party scene, with a travertine alfresco glowing in the dusk, an aqua-blue pool glimmering gently in front of the crowd of glittery bodies, and the house, a glorious, rambling mansion, a backdrop to this oozing, opulent wealth.

And the one character who didn't belong. Not because everyone else had decided she didn't, but because, long ago, *she* had made a decision that she didn't *want* to belong to this kind of milieu.

'She' became Adela, named for a student I never taught except tangentially, who also seemed to me to have made the decision not to belong for her own reasons.

I fell in love with the characters, the world, and the journey that would take Adela to that climactic moment at the poolside.

I tried to write the poolside scene… and instead wound up writing three stories in a week about her beginnings, her origin story—or at least, the beginnings of her relationship with the main male character.

This story is the second; the first is *Anamata*, which is Inklet #47, and the third story will be Inklet #78. Maybe, by then, I will have returned to this world and written some more stories for you to enjoy, so we—you and I alike—can come to understand how and why this young woman ends up by the side of an aquamarine pool at twilight, staring with equal parts bemusement and wistfulness at a party she is present at but not really present for, sharing a second dose of Anamata with a man she hated as a boy.

* I shan't make the assumption that everyone knows what 'Dramione' means: it means fanfiction based on the Harry Potter universe, but an alternate version where Hermione ends up with Draco.

Read more by Amy Laurens!

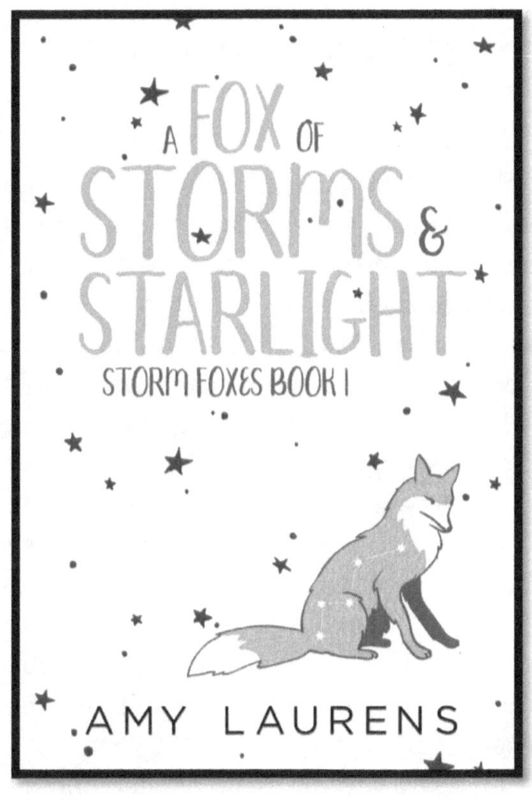

A FOX OF STORMS AND STARLIGHT

CHAPTER ONE

SIX YEARS AGO, I SAVED a fox in the bush. It was only because my dog died. At the time, it felt like a pretty crappy bargain.

It was the first day of autumn—not by the calendar, but by the fresh bite in the morning air, the golden quality of the light as it lit the main road through town in the mid-afternoon.

Sailor was a big, black shaggy thing, something like a Newfoundland, a lively shadow in the golden light, and I was eleven.

I'm sorry to be starting any story this way, but the fact of the matter is, this where it all began.

I'll spare you the awful details. Enough to say that Sailor had got out of the yard somehow, and had been hit by a smallish truck careening down the highway that split our tiny town in two as it blatantly ignored the speed limit.

I saw it happen.

And although I cradled him in my lap as the smell of burnt-out brakes and hot asphalt and turning leaves filled my nose, his giant, furry black head all of him I could hold, there was nothing I could do.

There was nothing anyone could do.

I knew that, but it didn't stop the knot of frustration and guilt in my chest, or the taste of bile in the back of my throat every time I closed my eyes and saw the truck hitting him, again and again and again.

It took years for that vision to fade.

But that evening, only a few hours after it had happened, everything still felt fresh, and raw.

Sunny, my sister, was only nine at the time. She cried for hours, just sobbing like she'd never breathe right again.

I'd cried a little, at the scene with Sailor's head lying in my lap as his big, brown eye stared up at nothing.

It had been mercifully fast, there was that.

And the driver had copped a massive fine—speeding, reckless driving, I think they even defected his truck—and came to visit us later, a big, pot-bellied man standing on our front verandah, shuffling his royal blue cap round and round and round in his hands as he apologised.

But that evening, with Sunny sobbing her heart out on the couch in the living room and Mum and Dad trying desperately to console her as dinner burned on the stove, I couldn't cry, even though the acrid scent of burning soy sauce, scorching brown sugar and smoking rice wine from the marinade prickled the back of my throat and the corners of my eyes.

I was the eldest, and I had to be responsible.

Possibly, if I'd been just a little more responsible, Sailor wouldn't have died.

So I slipped out the glass slider from the family room to the deck while Sunny cried, glancing up at the two storeys of our moody grey house behind me before jumping down the three steps from the rail-less deck to the lawn, and set out for the gate in the back fence.

I couldn't cry, and I didn't want to add anything to an already chaotic and stressful situation inside—but I couldn't stay there, either.

In the gaps between the gum trees to the west, the sky tinged to red and gold at the horizon, the sun sinking slowly into oblivion. I'm pretty sure I didn't know the word oblivion back then, but I knew what it meant, how it felt—and I craved it, desperately.

Anything would be better than the gaping hole in my chest.

And so, because I didn't know where to find it or how to get there, I stalked through the bush, pushing myself until I breathed hard and my lungs ached and sweat ringed me, chasing the way that hard exercise elevated me over my constantly looping thoughts.

Directly above, dark, heavy clouds obscured the sky, and the air was thick, heavy, humid.

Beneath the smell of dry gum leaves and even drier dirt, I could catch a hint of ozone, and occasionally the wind turned cool for a breath as it gusted against my skin, promising a late evening storm.

I strode harder, faster, outpacing the video looping in my mind of the truck's impact.

When the first drops of rain spat at me from out of the sky, I barely noticed. My skin was filmed with sweat, slick and salty, and the peppering of rainwater barely added to it.

That was at first.

But within minutes, it became clear that those first pattering spits had been the early foreshadowing of a storm darker and more intense than any I remembered.

Thunder rolled across the sky, distant and grumbling at first, a lazy background chorus to the rhythmic melody of the rain as it splattered down on grey-green leaves and red-tinged twigs, turning the silvered bark of an old, dead gum to deep grey and making the spiky, tussocky grass seem oddly luminescent in the dying light.

I stood under a grey gum with stains down its trunk that the rain was turning orange, arms wrapped around myself, shivering hard—and for the briefest instant, thought about not going home.

Mum and Dad would pitch a fit.

And I had to be responsible.

I turned, dark t-shirt plastered to my skin, dark hair sticking to my face and clinging to my neck, and began trudging my way back.

The storm closed over properly, clouds rolling over the horizon and cutting off the thin scythe of blood-coloured sunset, making the bush dark and unwelcoming in the premature night.

Lightning flashed.

Thunder cracked hot on its heels.

I jumped—and stared hard at the gap between two ghost-barked trees, where for a second, I was sure I'd seen a pair of eyes.

Nothing moved.

Nothing except the drenching rain, anyway, weighing down the branches that tossed fitfully in the wind.

My pulse slowly calmed.

The rumours we'd all grown up with, indoctrinated since both, spoke of something strange and dark… but in the forest north of here, in the pines, the plantation—not here, not in the natural, native bush.

I shivered.

The smell of wet dirt and soaked bark rose around me, undercut by eucalypt and ozone.

If anything had the power to wash away the hurt inside me, this storm was it. I tipped my face to the sky, imagining that the rain washing over me had the ability to wash me inside as well, and the raindrops splattered hard on my cheekbones, my chin, my tightly closed eyelids.

More lightning. More thunder, cracking over the constant hiss of the falling rain.

And in the distance, something eerie, lifting the hairs on the back of my neck: a strange kind of high-pitched howl, a cry that rang with moonlight and distance, cutting straight through the noise of the storm.

Bolts of lightning streaked across the sky—one—two—three—in the space of half a second, followed immediately by a growling crack of thunder so immense it vibrated in my chest.

I ducked down instinctively into a crouch.

There, in the corner of my eye...

I froze, crouched with my arms over my head.

The strange cries came again—and they were closer.

I stared hard at the place, low to the ground, where I was sure I'd seen something small, maybe the size of a cat.

Flash. Growl.

Rain spitting down.

There. Right there. A small animal, pointy ears, light coloured chin and throat...

The strange, eerie cries came a third time, and my heart pounded fiercely. Whatever was making the noise, it was close. Really close.

The little creature across from me reacted too, flattening itself to the ground.

My jaw twitched.

My heart pounded.

My fingertips bit into my upper arms.

Stay? Go?

Run? Freeze?

The hairs on my neck prickled again and goosebumps broke out all over me.

Cold dread formed a knot in my stomach.

Something was coming.

Something worse than the storm.

I had to get home.

I made it halfway to standing—and a series of strange, awful noises made me freeze again. They were sharp, clacking, squealing sounds, like someone knocking two echoing stones against each other, interspersed with high-pitched yowling...

The creature in the darkness screamed.

I threw my back against the gumtree behind me, pressing hard against it.

My heart hammered.

I peered back and forth in the dark, eyes wide.

Rain drenched down, but my throat was dry.

My pulse pounded faster.

The little creature screamed again—and as lightning flashed, I saw it on its back, legs slashing wildly as something attacked.

The awful, clicking-yowling noises sounded right in front of me.

I slapped my hands over my ears, gasping. Water ran down my face, getting into my mouth, my eyes.

It was hurting.

Whatever the small thing was, it was getting hurt, and I'd seen enough animals hurting today.

Something in my chest snapped.

I flung myself across the ground, leaping a couple of tussocks and a fallen branch before I crashed to my knees.

I crawled closer, desperate, gasping for air through the heavy curtains of rain.

I couldn't see it. Where?

Somewhere here, near the base of that tree…

The yowling screeched right next to my ear. I cowered against the ground, spiky grass pricking my face, wet-earth smell smothering me—but now, there was a strange mustiness too, a cousin to wet-dog smell.

At the next flash of lightning, I saw it.

The creature was a fox—and something barely visible was attacking it, only the gleam of eye or flicker of teeth visible in the gloom.

But the damage was real enough.

The little fox's side had been opened right up, and in the bright, stark flashes of heavenly electricity, the blood was dark, thinned by the constant rain.

No. No more animals were going to die today.

Not when this time, I could do something about it.

I snatched at a branch on the ground that turned out to be more of a glorified twig, and launched myself toward the creature.

I had no idea what was attacking it, but I screamed and waved my handful of twiggy leaves anyway, batting them in the air over the fox like I knew what I was doing.

The horrible clacking cries ceased abruptly.

With one long, low rumble, the rain began to ebb.

I poised, waiting.

But nothing came.

The attackers were gone.

Still gasping for air, pulse galloping in my throat, I sat next to the fox and shifted it carefully into my lap, realising as I tasted salt that I was crying.

I huddled over, trying to shelter the poor creature from the slackening rain, running my fingers over its wiry cheek—over and over and over and over.

"Please," I sobbed, throat tight and aching, chest constricted. "Please. Please don't die. Please."

Please, I prayed to anything that might be listening. *No more death. Not today.*

Not today.

Another gust of cool air washed over the clearing, taking the last of the rain with it—and lifting the goose-bumps on my arms again.

And as it did, I could have sworn I heard a voice. *Neither do I wish him to die now.*

I shivered, drawing the fox close, like it was a stuffed animal I could hug for comfort—its comfort or mine, I couldn't say. I glanced around the dripping bush, eyes wide. The rumours spoke of an evil presence, and I could easily believe that might be what had attacked the fox.

But a voice? No one had ever mentioned a voice.

There was nothing to be seen, and anyway the voice had sounded kindly— and didn't want the fox to die.

Assuming I hadn't just imagined it, of course. Which, half-drowned by grief, the other half drowned by the storm... An over-active imagination seemed highly likely.

Can you fix him? I thought it hard, though, just in case someone really was listening.

Something shifted in my lap.

Around us, the world stilled, dazed from the storm, but also something more, something watching, something waiting, as the bush held its collective breath.

The only sound was the occasional drip of rainwater from the gum leaves onto a fallen log—no insects, no wind, no rustling of leaves.

Just… stillness.

And the fox, who shivered in my lap.

The clouds tore open, revealing a ragged triangle of stars that glittered in the fox's eye as it blinked open and stared up at me.

My chest snagged.

My throat ached from crying, and a headache was forming in the back of my head.

But the fox blinked up at me—alive.

I ran a finger down it again, from nose to cheek to ear to shoulder, all the way down its side to its thick, bushy tail—and the wound in its side began to close.

Laboriously, it hauled itself to its front legs.

I tried to stop it—"No, it's okay, you can stay here, I'll look after you"—but it lifted its top lip to show half-hearted teeth, and staggered away.

As it did, I thought perhaps its fur began to shrink.

And suddenly, it looked larger in the night—as large as a dog, as large as Sailor...

But I blinked, and it was just a trick of the light, because the creature that darted away into the bushes like nothing was wrong at all was clearly a fox, the size of a large cat or maybe a small beagle, and nothing more.

And if something screamed in the night not long afterward, and the cry sounded horribly, horribly human?

Well.

I was halfway back toward home again by then, and I pressed my fingertips to my lower eyelids and prayed my parents wouldn't murder me for getting home so late.

Keep reading! Head to
www.inkprintpress.com/amylaurens/
stormfoxes/fox/
to buy your copy now!

ABOUT THE AUTHOR

AMY LAURENS is an Australian author of fantasy fiction for all ages. She has written the award-winning portal-fantasy *Sanctuary* series about Edge, a 13-year-old girl forced to move to a small country town because of witness protection (the first book is *Where Shadows Rise*), the humorous fantasy *Kaditeos* series, following newly graduated Evil Overlord Mercury as she attempts to acquire a castle, the young adult series *Storm Foxes*, about love and magic and family in small town Australia, and a whole host of non-fiction.

INKLET #055
Allure
AMY LAURENS

INKLET #056
The LIES We KNOW
LIANA BROOKS

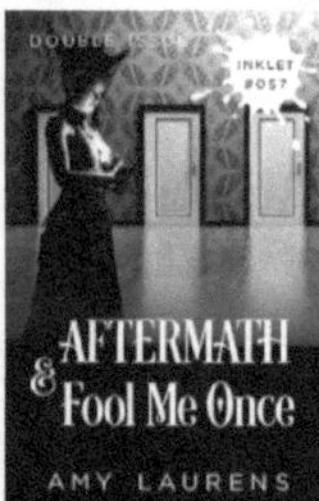

DOUBLE ISSUE
INKLET #057
AFTERMATH & Fool Me Once
AMY LAURENS

INKLET #058
Purity
An Age Of Unicorns Story
AMY LAURENS

INKLET #059
Saved
AMY LAURENS

INKLET #060
A Kiss is the Secret
AMY LAURENS

INKLET #061
A Changing Tides Story
Fire Bright
AMY LAURENS

INKLET #062
Hades AND Persephone
LIANA BROOKS

INKLET #063
Just So Long As You're Happy
AMY LAURENS

INKLET #064
Theft Of A Lifetime
LIANA BROOKS

INKLET #065
Shoe
AMY LAURENS

INKLET #066
Published AUTHOR
LIANA BROOKS

DOUBLE ISSUE
INKLET #067
THE REMARKABLE INSIGHT OF JELLYBEANS & Understanding
AMY LAURENS

INKLET #068
Desperate Measures
AMY LAURENS

INKLET #069
Rock-a-bye
LIANA BROOKS

INKLET #070
the Other Carly
AMY LAURENS

INKLET #071
It's By Bioluminescent Light
AMY LAURENS

INKLET #072
Even Villains Grant Wishes
A Heroes & Villains Story
LIANA BROOKS